Clara

THE LOST PUPPY
Dotty DETECTIVE

HarperCollins *Children's Books*

First published in Great Britain by HarperCollins
Children's Books in 2017
HarperCollins *Children's Books*
is a division of HarperCollins*Publishers* Ltd,
1 London Bridge Street, London, SE1 9GF

The HarperCollins website address is: www.harpercollins.co.uk

1

Text and illustrations © Clara Vulliamy 2017

ISBN 978-0-00-824837-6

Clara Vulliamy asserts the moral right to be identified as the
author and illustrator of the work.

Printed and bound in England by Clays Ltd, St Ives plc

MIX
Paper from
responsible sources

FSC C007454
www.fsc.org

FSC™ is a non-profit international organisation established to promote
the responsible management of the world's forests. Products carrying the
FSC label are independently certified to assure consumers that they come
from forests that are managed to meet the social, economic and
ecological needs of present and future generations,
and other controlled sources.

Find out more about HarperCollins and the environment at
www.harpercollins.co.uk/green

For my dear friend Kate Jessop,
with love

Read the whole series:

This book belongs to...

DOT

and McClusky

SUNDAY

This is me – Dot!

And this is TOP DOG, McClusky.

There is something *extremely important* you need to know …

Me and McClusky and our best pal Beans (who is in my class at school) are SUPER-SECRET AGENTS with our very own detective agency – the JOIN THE DOTS DETECTIVES! There is no mystery we cannot solve, however dastardly difficult.

But there is **NO TIME** to tell you more about that now!

JOIN THE DOTS DETECTIVES

I **J**U**MP** up out of bed and eat my favourite breakfast cereal (which is Honey Nut Crunchers) at *supersonic* speed

CRUNCH

SLURP.

I am having kittens

with nerves...

…because today I am trying out for the **HIGHFIELD HARRIERS**, our local running team!

Setting off for the park now – me, Mum, McClusky and the twins (my brother and sister, Alf and Maisy).

Grandpa George is waiting for us at the park entrance. He takes the twins over to the swings so Mum can concentrate on **cheering** for me.

I'm actually a pretty *fast* runner.

Me and Mum do running training together every weekend.

I try my *absolute* hardest…

* PHEW. * It goes **OK!**

Really hope I get in.

McClusky has a busy morning in
the park too, meeting up with his
friend, a big silly dog called Geoffrey.
McClusky has a SERIOUSLY
HECTIC social life.

Geoffrey belongs to Amy who is also in my class at school.

He is HUGE – nearly as tall as her!

McClusky and Geoffrey
go **crazy** with joy
to see each other, chasing round and round like lunatics

and playing **hide-and-seek** in the bushes.

McClusky spends all afternoon asleep in his bed, **EXHAUSTED.** But at teatime, just one rustle of the WaggyTail dog food bag and he's awake and up like a rocket.

Back in my room, which is also Join the Dots Detectives HQ – TOP SECRET! I'm packing my bag and getting ready for school tomorrow.

I have a quick tidy up of my stationery collection, which let me tell you is amazing. Pens, stickers, paperclips, pencil-toppers, notebooks … and dots on EVERYTHING!!

Looking forward to trying out my new super-sticky glow-in-the-dark dotty sticky tape sometime soon.

This is going to be a GOOD week – it's nearly the end of term and that means it's nearly the summer holidays! AND next Saturday it's the school summer fair!!!

Monday

Arriving at school, and there's a
FANTASTIC surprise waiting for us…

Joe Buckley has brought in his new
sausage dog puppy, Chipolata!

She is SOOOO
 CUTE!!!

It is her *first ever* outing. Puppies have to stay at home indoors for the first few weeks, but Joe has been telling us ALL about her.

Joe is not the only one who is excited…

McClusky and Geoffrey are over the moon to make a new friend!

The three dogs are tied to the railings because they aren't allowed in the playground.

Chipolata is VERY wriggly and full of bounce.

She gets all tangled up with McClusky who starts barking and that sets off Geoffrey too.

What a **crazy** bunch the school gate gang are!

WOOF!

WOOF!

WOOF!

23

Lining up to go into the classroom, Joe tells us about some *funny* things Chipolata has done while she's been settling in to her new home.

"The other day, she hid in a cardboard tube and got **stuck**. She loves getting in the washing basket, too. One time she burrowed right inside my mum's jumper and got trapped in the sleeve!"

Joe longed for a puppy for ages and ages but his family had to save up – sausage dogs are VERY expensive. What a difference to McClusky – he came from an animal rescue centre!

Certificate of Adoption

This certifies that .... Dot ....

has officially adopted .. McClusky ......

I promise to give my dog
a forever home
of love, care and fun.
I will be his best friend always.

In class, we are all
super-excited
because of the **summer fair**.

Our teacher, Mr Dickens, tells us
that our class will be in charge of
Pets Corner. He asks us all about
 our pets. "Pets Corner will have a
guessing competition," he says.
"Guess the height of Geoffrey,
for instance ... Any other ideas?"

"Guess the length of Chipolata!" says Joe.

"You'll *never* guess my guinea pig's name!" Nadia calls out.

Roly-Poly?

Mr Squeak?

?

Gordon?

Cheeky?

Caramel?

?

?

Bubbles?

?

"How about guess the **weight** of my STICK insect!" shouts Frankie Logan.

"I've got another one – how many biscuits in a

BIG

bag of dog food!" says Amy. "You won't *believe* how many Geoffrey gets through."

"Visitors to **Pets Corner** can pay for guesses, and the closest answers to each question will win a **PRIZE**," Mr Dickens tells us.

I'm not sure what visitors could guess about McClusky. He's not extra TALL or SHORT or long. I'll have a think.

Beans says "I WISH I had a pet!" He still misses Norman, the earwig he met on the school trip to **Adventure Camp**.

"I'm going to design the world's **BEST** robot pet," he says.

Beans is **brilliant** at inventing things.

this doodle is by Beans!

AERIAL SO NEVER GETS LOST

LIGHT-UP COLLAR

CARRIES SNACKS

5-SPEED TAIL-WAGGING

NIGHT VISION

TV SCREEN

EXTRA-LONG DISTANCE SMELLING

EXTENDABLE FOR GOING THROUGH PUDDLES

6 LEGS FOR SUPER-SPEEDY WALKIES

We are all chatting about what we will do at the fair.

"There's going to be a **popcorn** machine!" says Fiyaz.

"AND a **bouncy** castle!" adds Kirstie.

"I'll be playing my trumpet in the brass band performance," says Marcus. Then we all **loudly** pretend to be playing in the brass band too … until Frankie is *too* **wild** with his imaginary trombone and knocks over his chair.

TOOT! TOOT!

"Righto, you noisy crew," says Mr D, "we need to get down to some work now."

We don't mind though because this work will be fun...

Mr D tells us that this week, to get in the mood for the fair, we will learn about **South American carnivals!**

TUEsdAy

At the school gates Chipolata is even more *wriggly*. She keeps getting in everybody's way and tripping people up.

Kirstie's dad laughs and says,
"She shouldn't be left lying around –
someone might STEAL her!"

"AWWW she's so lovely," says
Milo's mum. "She would make such a
cosy hot-water bottle!"

At lunchtime, Mrs Bagshott our head
teacher asks for helpers to put up
bunting all around the playground.

Me, Beans and Amy have a *really*

loooong...

piece of bunting, blue and yellow,
which are the school colours. We tie
it up on to the railings, as high as we
can reach.

It's a bit higher at one end and lower at the other, because Amy is tallest, then Beans, then me.

But it all looks really good.

Getting **SO IMPATIENT** for the day of the fair to arrive!

In Music, Mr D shows us a film in the hall about Samba drumming from Brazil. It is **SO cool**.

We have a go ourselves, with drums and also tambourines, bells and whistles. VERY noisy!

Mr Meades come
in to sweep ...
and does a little
dance with his
broom.

As we are
packing our bags to go home,
Mr Dickens says, "You'll NEVER
GUESS what I will be doing at the
fair! It's going to be a

BIG surprise..."

He is *always* teasing us!

After tea, I am relaxing in my room and thinking about the summer holidays.

Me and my family are not actually going away anywhere but we will be having lots of brilliant *DAY TRIPS.*

Beans is staying at home too, so Mum says he can join in with some of our outings if he likes. Top of our list is the open-air swimming pool, a picnic at Westbury Farm Park …

AND Beans's Auntie Celia says she will take us **GO-KARTING!**

WOOO Hoooo!!!

We are in a

HUGE

rush

to get to school today. First Maisy
forgets the dragon drawing she
wanted to bring to Nursery so we
have to go back for it ...

And then Alf suddenly remembers
a very important pebble he wanted
to bring, so we have to go back
AGAIN...

And *at last* I arrive at school.

In registration we are **all** trying to guess what Mr D's surprise is.

"Juggling?"

"NO."

"Doing a *dance* with Mrs Bagshott?"

"NO."

"Giving everybody **FREE** ice creams?"

"NO."

We have **NO IDEA** what it could be.

In Science, me, Beans, Fiyaz and Nadia are in a group for our South American-rainforest-animals project.

We head over to the ICT suite to research the most **unusual** animals we can find – caimans, anteaters, civets ...

caiman

anteater

civet

We choose a capybara to focus on, which is a *bit* like a guinea pig but

HUGE.

HUGE!

PRETTY SMALL

Now THAT would be an exciting guest in **Pets Corner!!!**

! ! ! ! ! ! ! ! !

It's absolute **CHAOS** in the playground at going-home time. The **bouncy** castle is being delivered by van. Food for the BBQ and the big bag of dog food for **Pets Corner** is being carried into Mr Meades's storeroom and the stage is being assembled.

STORE
ROOM

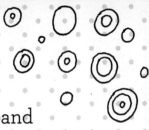

In all the muddle of crowds and people *coming* and *going* it takes me ages to find Mum! But when we come out of the school gate to fetch McClusky…

Chipolata has GONE.

All that's left is her lead attached to the railings.

Joe is *really* upset, but his mum says, "Don't worry, Joe, we'll soon find her. She couldn't have got very far on those little legs."

Everybody promises to keep their
EYES PEELED.

"Which way did she go, McClusky?"
I ask. But he isn't listening. He seems
more interested in Mr Meades
carrying a **huge** box of burgers
across the playground.

We can't help worrying about Chipolata
as we walk back from school. She is
too young to know her way home.
I ask Mum to text Joe's mum:

Any luck?

but the answer comes back:

Not yet.

We search every front garden and
every bush on the way home, but
there is **no sign** of Chipolata
anywhere.

On the corner of the street where I go one way and Beans goes the other, there is just time for a super-hasty **JOIN THE DOTS DETECTIVES** meeting.

"This is a *REAL* mystery," I whisper, "and we have the *perfect* detectively skills to find Chipolata!"

"YES!" whispers Beans. "We have already solved lots of cases AND we've got McClusky to help us!"

We decide that the first thing to do is look for clues and find witnesses. Somebody *must* have seen her.

Wherever she is, we will find her.

The **JOIN THE DOTS DETECTIVES** are **ON THE CASE!**

Back at Dot HQ, I get to work making a LOST poster. This calls for my very best pens from my stationery collection.

LOST!
SAUSAGE DOG
PUPPY CALLED
CHIPOLATA

It needs to go across three pieces of paper, because Chipolata is so long: one for her tail end, one for her middle section and one for her nose end.

IF YOU SEE HER
PLEASE BRING HER
BACK TO JOE
AT OAKFIELD SCHOOL

After tea, Mum is **experimenting** in the kitchen.

She is trying out a **new** recipe for cupcakes, which she will be baking for the fair.

There are bowls of different icing on the table – **peanut butter,** mint choc chip, *Turkish delight,* **strawberries and cream** …

Me and the twins help by each bringing a teaspoon and trying them. It takes *quite a few spoonfuls* for us to give our final definite opinions on which we like **best**.

I have a

brilliant

idea!

I ask Mum for a cupcake as a special treat in my lunchbox, but *really* it is to send a secret message to Beans.

I borrow a glitter-writing icing tube, and write a secret message on the cake.

Thursday

On the way to school, I put up the LOST poster. It sticks up really well with my *glow-in-the-dark dotty sticky tape!*

We search in bushes and gardens again, calling out Chipolata's name.

CHIPOLATA!

CHIPOLATA!

CHIPOLATA!

In class, Joe is sad. Chipolata hasn't turned up yet.

We try to cheer him up. "Don't worry, she'll be home again really soon, you'll see!"

At breaktime, I give Beans the cake.

Super-speedily, we split the cupcake into two and eat it, so no one else can read it.

We are in **the Lookout**, which is our secret meeting place in the playground.

the playground

the Lookout

nature corner

Mr Meades store-room

the hall

School office

Mrs B's office

stage for the fair

classrooms

Beans says, "You *could* have just told me that we needed to meet here – why the cupcake?"

But I say, "It's **good** to keep practising our detectively skills – and it's a lot more *fun* to write a SECRET MESSAGE you can EAT!"

"It's a lot more tasty, too," agrees Beans. He has a blob of mint choc chip icing on his nose.

"Now let's make a map of the area, so we can do a proper search," I say. Beans is

SO CLEVER

at maps.

We work out that as Chipolata can only walk a little way on her short legs, she couldn't have got far.

We draw a circle to show the search area.

Inside the circle we put a **star** next to the *special* places of interest we think she could be.

"What about a list of possible witnesses?" I ask. "People to speak to who might have seen something …"

Mums and dads

Paws Awhile owner

Butcher

Pink Vanilla Café owner

Park keeper

Ice-cream van driver

67

We are very pleased with our map – it's a good place to start.

For today's spellings we play "silent letters snakes and ladders".

We roll a dice and move along the snakes and ladders board. Every time we land on a square there is a spelling question with a silent letter in it to answer, like the "K" in "knot".

Get it right, you go up the ladder.

Get it wrong – *down the snake!*

It's **SO TRICKY!**

I get a ladder because I got "gnome"
right (HOORAY!) but a snake with
~~rubarb~~ "rhubarb".

Amy who sits at my table is first
to get all of hers right. Beans is
struggling with "gnu", and Frankie
Logan isn't really trying at all …

He is doing an impression of a gnat
and sends a pencil pot flying.

"Calamity custard!" says Mr D.
"There's never anything silent about
you, Frankie!"

At lunchtime, me and Beans sit with
Joe. We show him the map of the
search area, places of interest and
possible witnesses. He thinks it's
really great. We all share my mango
slices.

In Science, me and my Rainforest group are finding FACTS about camouflage. It's AMAZING how clever some animals are.

Here is a chameleon *pretending* to be a leaf!

At going-home time, Joe shows the
map to his mum. She says, "Thank you
so much, this is REALLY HELPFUL."

"We want to search with you!" I say.
"Can we, Mum?"

Mum says we should all help to
search. Beans and his dad are keen.
Lots of other parents at the school
gates overhear and agree to help too.

Mr D asks, "What can I do?" And I
say, "We need leaflets to hand out!"
He borrows a photograph from Joe's

Mum, and our map, and rushes back into the school office. A few minutes later, he returns with lots of leaflets.

MISSING!

Have YOU seen
Chipolata?

Last seen at Oakfield School
PLEASE CALL!

We split up into groups to search. Our group is me, Beans, Frankie, our parents and the twins and McClusky too, of course.

Heading up to the high street first. We call in at each shop, asking if **anyone** has seen Chipolata.

Everybody we speak to is very kind and sympathetic, but **no one** has seen her.

We leave a leaflet at each place, to go in the window.

Now we are in the park. Luckily it's a summer evening and still light, which gives us more time.

I think back to Sunday when McClusky was playing with Geoffrey, trying to remember all the places that dogs especially like.

We search high and l o w

although as she had such little legs there's not much point in high.

"I don't think she could be up a tree, Frankie!!!" I say.

Even the twins are doing their bit, looking in the tall grass and flowerbeds.

Could she be camouflaged somehow? I look closely at **muddy** places and soil which are dark brown like Chipolata.

Then Beans remembers something. "Joe told us she got stuck in a **cardboard tube** – and the sleeve of a jumper! Look out for long thin things, everybody!"

There's the gardener's hosepipe,
but that's too small. The tunnel to crawl
through in the playground, but that's
too big.

No sign of Chipolata **anywhere.**

And there is something **very strange** about McClusky. He doesn't show any interest in looking. He pulls on his lead to go back the way we came, *whining*.

He is being lazy and wants to go home! I am completely mystified – doesn't he CARE?

Mum texts Joe's mum and the other search parties. They decide to call it a day and try again tomorrow, so we all head home.

 Tea is huge bowls of spaghetti Bolognese. We are all SO hungry.

At bedtime, I look in my **FRED FANTASTIC'S CRAZY CRIME CAPERS** book for inspiration.

Fred Fantastic is an **ACE** detective on TV. With his cool sidekick Flo, there is no case, however fiendishly tricky, they cannot solve. They search the mean streets of the big city for clues, and never give up until they find the evidence they need.

The **JOIN THE DOTS DETECTIVES** think that **FRED FANTASTIC'S** Five Golden Rules for solving a mystery are *ALWAYS* really useful...

 1 STAY FROSTY.
Always be on the lookout.

FOLLOW THAT HUNCH!
If you've got a funny feeling,
you may be on to something
important.

 USE YOUR NOODLE.
Think!

 **LOOK FOR A LIGHT-BULB
MOMENT.**
A sudden genius idea.

 GET PROOF.
You **MUST** have the evidence
before you can solve your
case.

I read a story about how Fred
travelled all the way

ACROSS
AMERICA

on a Greyhound bus (which doesn't
have a greyhound driving it, it just
means it is very fast) in search
of the final piece of evidence in
his case, only to find it was in his
pocket all along.

I don't think this helps us much.

"**USE YOUR NOODLE**, *DOT!*" I say to myself.

What can we try next???

Friday

"COME ON – WE ARE GOING TO BE

LATE

FOR SCHOOL!"

Mum is saying.

But we are all waiting by the front door while she searches for her keys.

86

I am

rushing

through the school gate. McClusky tries to follow, LONGING to rush through the gate with me. It takes ALL Mum's strength to hold him back.

"Is it because you *really miss me* during the day, McClusky?" I ask him.

In the classroom, we are all talking about where we have been looking for Chipolata.

"I waited outside the butcher's for HOURS," says Marcus.

"The *butcher's,* Marcus??" we ask.

"I thought she would be looking for **sausages!**" he explains.

Laura (who is definitely NOT my friend usually) says she and her mum have been out looking too. I am really pleased she is joining in.

But still no sightings, no clues.

"Don't worry, Joe," we say, "she will turn up again really soon!"

But secretly we are thinking that she must be getting further and further away by now.

"If Chipolata was lost, someone would have seen her by now, surely?" Beans says to me quietly when Joe has walked away.

An **awful** thought starts to grow in my head.

What if she is not hiding but someone is *deliberately*

hiding her???

No time to talk about it now though – Mr D tells us to go to our places for quiet reading. I will have to wait until breaktime.

However down in the dumps
we are feeling, the **fair** must go on.

In Art we are making decorations
for **Pets Corner** out of coloured
paper and collage.

I fold a long piece of black paper into a concertina and cut out a cat shape.

When I open it up –

ta-DA!

– it's a garland of cats!

In PE, Mr D shows us how to dance the Bossa Nova.

I am always in a dance pair with Frankie. Although he is often crashing about in the classroom causing chaos, it turns out that he has *hidden talents*...

"**WOW,** Frankie," says Mr D, "you've got rhythm!"

At breaktime, I RUSH to the Lookout with Beans …

"Do you remember at the school gates, when Chipolata was really wriggly and kept tripping people up?" I ask Beans. "What was it that Kirstie's dad said??

"Someone might steal her!"

"OH NO – that's **TERRIBLE!**" says Beans. "She must be very valuable. Joe said she cost a lot of money …"

The more we think about it, the more convinced we are. What other explanation could there be? The case has now taken a disastrous, **VILLIANOUS** turn!

Chipolata has been STOLEN!!!!

"We must write a list of suspects," I say.

Kirstie's dad?
Milo's mum?
the bouncy castle van driver?
the BBQ delivery person?
someone just passing by?

Kirstie's dad?

He is at the top of the list!

Milo's mum?

"She would make a such a cosy hot-water bottle!" we heard her say.

Maybe *she* stole Chipolata?

But it could be someone we don't even know ... the bouncy castle van driver? The BBQ delivery person? Someone just passing by?

The worst thing is, it could be

anybody...

How **could** McClusky let Chipolata get stolen – Geoffrey yes, he's not too bright, but McClusky??

Heading back into class after breaktime, still *whispering* about our suspects and what our next move should be.

We are walking behind Mrs Bagshott and we overhear her saying, "I've got a new one, a **beautiful dark brown** – **so soft** and **so sweet!**"

We look at each other. Eyes **wide** with shock.

Could Mrs Bagshott be talking about Chipolata????

"We need to get as close to Mrs Bagshott as we can – find out more!" I say urgently to Beans.

Beans looks extremely nervous, but he nods his head: **YES.**

"FOLLOW THAT HUNCH, Dot!"
Beans says.

"STAY FROSTY, Beans!" I say.

In Art, we are finishing the decorations
for Pets Corner. But we can hardly
concentrate. I have accidentally drawn

THREE
EYES

on one of my paper cats without
thinking!

"We must get closer to Mrs Bagshott's office!" I whisper to Beans.

It is SO

SCARY

to spy on the head teacher (and she is quite scary anyway!!) but *the stakes are high*. We MUST save Chipolata, and do the right thing for Joe!

At lunchtime, we creep along the corridor and hide behind her office door …

"I'm terrified!" Beans whispers.
"What if she finds us spying on her?
We are going to be in **BIG**
TROUBLE!"

At first we can't hear anything clearly,
just muffled voices and the opening
and shutting of a cupboard drawer.
But *then* ...

"It's **so warm** and silky and SO
LONG!" Mrs Bagshott is saying.
"Someone just left it outside the
school. No one seems to want it.
I think I'll take it home and keep it!"

So it's **TRUE!**

MRS BAGSHOTT

STOLE

CHIPOLATA!!!!

We are completely *horrified.*

We hurry back to the classroom
before anyone sees us.

In Maths I am doing an extra-tricky worksheet on circumferences and diameters, which usually I LOVE, but today I just stare at the page, not even seeing.

At going-home time, I whisper to Beans, "This is our last chance to get Chipolata back! *Come on,* QUICK!"

We come out of the main door with everybody else, but then slip round the corner and duck down behind a low wall.

We creep along to just outside
Mrs Bagshott's office. My heart
is

THUMPING

in my chest.
But there's no turning back now!

We pop up and on tiptoe we can just
reach to see in through the window.

! ! ! ! ! ! ! !

And there she is, putting on her coat,
picking up her bag, and stroking …
a long **soft** *brown* …

SCARF,

with tiny rabbits
embroidered on it.

Our hearts sink into our boots,
hopes of finding Chipolata dashed.

"I was SO SURE we had the culprit," says Beans, as we walk home.

"We were **barking** up the wrong tree," I say.

This doesn't mean we were *actually* barking up a real tree ...

WOOF!

WOOF!

It means we followed the wrong lead and made a mistake.

I feel *terrible* about it. We were so sure we have the *perfect* detectively skills to find Chipolata, but so far –

NOTHING.

With every day that goes by I worry more and more about her.

For tea, Mum makes us peas and rice which is usually my favourite, but I hardly touch it. She has saved three

spare cupcakes especially for us but
I don't even
want one.

It's evening and I'm just fetching a
drink of water in the kitchen.

McClusky is **whining** and *whimpering*.
Is he trying to tell me something?

He pulls his bag of WaggyTail dog
food over to me and looks expectant.
His tail is *whirring* like a propeller.

"How *could* you think about **dinner** at a time like this, McClusky?!?"

 I just don't know what to do.

Poor puppy. And poor Joe!

Saturday

All morning I'm worrying about the fair. **Pets Corner** just won't be the same with Chipolata **missing**. We will be feeling sad about her the whole time. I'm sure Joe won't even want to be there.

McClusky does, though – he's been ready and waiting at the front door **since breakfast!**

I try some **tricky** wordsearches in my puzzle book to relax, but I just can't concentrate.

Mum gives us each a little bit of spending money for the fair. I pop it safely in my purse.

I have a purse shaped like an ice cream. Alf has a piglet purse and Maisy has a purse in the shape of a Tyrannosaurus Rex.

We arrive at school early to get
Pets Corner ready.

Me, Beans and Nadia help Mr D to
put up the enclosure and decorate it.

Mr Meades is busy

rushing to and fro,

bringing the BBQ food from his
storeroom and helping to inflate the
bouncy castle.

The school choir, recorder group and brass band are all practising different songs at the same time which makes a terrible noise!

Parents are setting up **exciting-looking** stalls, and there's a

delicious smell

wafting over from the **p°pcorn** machine.

As soon as McClusky is put inside the **Pets Corner** enclosure he tries desperately to J^{UMP} out. It must be his delight at actually being inside the playground at last. Maybe he wants to explore?

I am embarrassed by McClusky's
over-excitement in front of Joe.
"We didn't think you would come,"
we say to Joe.

"Would you like to hold my stick
insect?" asks Frankie kindly.

McClusky is looking at me
SO intensely.

"What *is* it, McClusky?" I ask him.

He has been acting so strangely
lately! It just doesn't make sense …

I think back to when he was *pulling* on his lead during the search and I thought he was being lazy and wanting to go home … but perhaps it wasn't *home* he was trying to drag us back to …

I remember when he tried to **rush** in though the school gate with me …

And then last night he was **desperately** trying to show me his bag of dog food …

The penny drops …

I have a **LIGHT-BULB MOMENT!**

"McClusky KNOWS where Chipolata is!"

I say to Beans.

"He has known right from the very start. He's been trying to tell us *all along* in his own doggy way, and we didn't realise!"

We let McClusky go and he takes off at great speed across the playground, barking loudly.

I **RUN** after him, and Beans runs

after me. (Lucky I've picked up some speed on my training with Mum!)

McClusky leads us straight to Mr Meades's storeroom. He carries on barking and barking outside the door…

And then we hear another dog barking back.

It's CHIPOLATA – she is INSIDE!

Will she be **hungry**, *frightened*, cold and miserable??

NO!

Chipolata is *extremely fine* and **happy**, snuggled up warmly under Mr Meades's old woolly jumper!

She must have been so cosily **fast asleep** she hadn't even noticed when Mr Meades came in and out fetching things for the fair. It was only McClusky's

VERY
LOUD

barking that finally woke her up.

She has been feasting on the **big** bag of dog food for the *"Guess How Many Biscuits"* competition, and drinking from a tub of water Mr Meades keeps for watering his geraniums.

She must have followed the food, slipped in unnoticed when the door was ajar and got shut in.

Mr Meades has been too busy and distracted to notice her.

Chipolata wasn't LOST OR STOLEN ...

She was right under our noses all along!

McClusky and Chipolata are SO HAPPY to see each other. There is LOTS of tail-wagging.

We take Chipolata over to Joe who is absolutely **on top of the world**.

Joe's mum rushes over. She is all smiles and everybody **hugs** everybody else.

Pets Corner is a

GREAT

SUCCESS –

who knew

that a stick insect weighs so little,

or that Nadia's guinea pig is called

waffles?

86 cm

7g

Waffles!

Guessing the number of biscuits isn't going to be **too challenging** as its clear to see there are only a few left in the dog-food bag.

"Lucky for Chipolata it's her length and not the circumference of her belly that is being guessed!" we whisper to each other SECRETLY.

I wasn't sure what visitors to **Pets Corner** could guess about McClusky, but I do know now. It is to guess his extra-special genius skill.

He is SO CLEVER

and has a brilliant nose for sniffing out the clues – the **ACE DETECTIVE** who found the lost puppy!

You can measure a tall dog and weigh a stick insect and count the dog biscuits, but you just cannot measure how much of a star McClusky has been in the **JOIN THE DOTS DETECTIVES**. He was giving us messages that were the *vital clues* all along.

"I am SO SO SORRY, McClusky," I say to him. "How could I ever have doubted you?"

He gives me a lick as if to say, "That's OK! We are a **GREAT** *team!*"

Me, Beans and Joe go around the **fair** visiting all the stalls.

Joe's mum buys us each an

extra-big bag

of fresh **popcorn**,

and a NEW squeaky toy for McClusky.

squeak!

I win a small panda bear key-ring at the Teddy Tombola, and Beans has his face painted as an **ALIEN**.

We have lots of tries at the **HAIRY HEDGEHOG** game...

You pick out one of prickles (which are really made from cocktail sticks) and the ones with a coloured end get a **prize**. Joe wins some **sherbet fruit candies** and shares them with us.

The twins are having a great time too. They spend **ages** on the **bouncy** castle, and Mum buys them a daisy each at the plant stall.

Grandpa George makes *several* visits to the afternoon-tea stall for strawberry cream scones.

We watch the **karate display**,
the **choir**, the **brass band**,
the **recorders** …

And now there are loud whoops and
cheers and here comes Mr Dickens …

He is a

ONE-MAN
BAND!!!

He plays a squeezebox and a mouth
organ and cymbals and a **HUGE**

drum *all at the same time*, and sings some **VERY** funny songs.

So *that* was his surprise!

"What a day!" says Mum, as we sit on the sofa together before bedtime. The phone rings ...

Some good news! I HAVE got into the **HIGHFIELD HARRIERS!**

YESSS!!!

I am on CLOUD NINE ...

Another case solved.

What will the next fiendishly tricky mystery be?

Have you read?

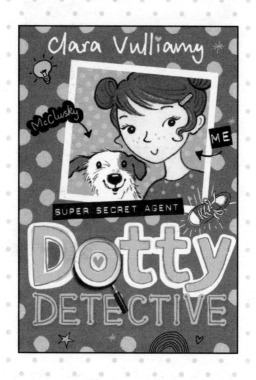

When someone seems set on sabotaging the school show, Dot is determined to find out how, and save the day!

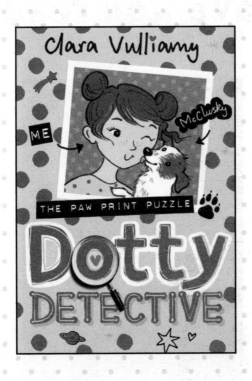

When Dot starts hearing strange noises
at night, Beans is convinced there has to
be something SPOOKY afoot. But, before
they can be certain, Dot and Beans must
GET PROOF.

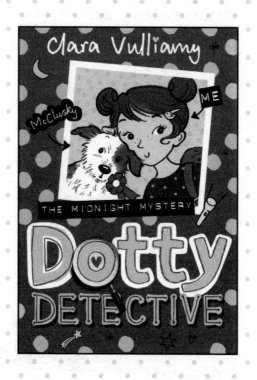

Dot and Beans can't wait for their school
trip to Adventure Camp where they will do
lots of exciting adventure activities and
may even win the Adventurers' Prize!
But why is someone trying to spoil the fun?

Join Dot, Beans and McClusky
on their next case...

LOOK OUT FOR ANOTHER

Dotty
DETECTIVE

coming soon...